THE THINGS THAT CHARM US

A Collection of Short Stories, Poems, and Essays

N. K. Carlson

CONTENTS

DEDICATION

To Haley, my model of delight.

ACKNOWLEDGEMENTS

This book has been a long time coming. A huge thanks to my wife, Haley for all of her valuable reading and feedback work. She also designed the cover for this book! Thanks to my parents for giving me a love of reading from an early age. Thank you to my teachers at Rockland Elementary School who gave me blank books to write stories in. Thank you to my teachers in middle school and high school for helping me to grow as a reader and a writer. Thank you to friends and family who read my early blogging efforts while in college. Thank you to the professors at Logsdon Seminary who helped me become a better writer and to read scripture through the lens of delight. And lastly, thank you reader, for taking the time to pick up this work. I hope that you find it simply delightful.

THE FORGOTTEN VIRTUE

Dear Reader,

What you hold in your hands is a book I never intended to write. Sometimes that leads to a good book and I hope that this is one of those cases.

You will find in these pages short stories, poems, and essays. That is a strange assortment, but I think you will find that they fit together. There is something here for everyone.

For a few years I have had this idea that we (take 'we' to mean whatever you want, Americans, Christians, humans, etc.) are missing something. There is something vitally important that we have forgotten that we must find again and soon. At first I thought that missing thing was kindness. There does seem to be a shortness of kindness in our world. If there were more kindness we should all be happier. But the thing that is missing is deeper than kindness. Kindness is the thing that springs forth, the water from the well. What we are missing is the well itself.

We are not living a charmed life. We as a species are at the height of our technological prowess, and only going upward, but we are missing something. Social media connects us in ways never before known. Yet in our connectedness, we are more alone and lonely than ever before.

Our work, our vocation, is drudgery toward the grave. We clock in and out and we miss the meaning of our actions. We live meaningless lives, unmoored, adrift with no anchor.

As a two-thousand-year-old Jewish Rabbi said, there are wars and rumors of wars. We are in conflict with one another over land and resources. Sometimes the conflict is simply a matter of hatred of the other side. Many people in our world lack the food they need to survive. Here in America, and in many other parts of the world, politics divide us, brother from brother, neighbor from neighbor. People die of gun violence and cancer. As I said above, there is a general lack of kindness, a nastiness of people toward others. We are quick to lash out and slow to hold our tongues. To sum it up, we have the distinct feeling that there is more. There is something we are missing.

That missing piece is the forgotten virtue of delight. Human beings can be quite delightful creatures, but so many of us live our lives far, far away from delight. The simple reason humans can be delightful is that we were created for delight. In the beginning, God made everything and planted a garden full of every type of fruit imaginable. And it was delightful. Delight is what we were made for and ever since the Garden of Eden, we have been searching for delight.

Many of us seek delight and settle for pleasure. Delight is wonder, awe and love. Pleasure is that which is temporary and seeks to approximate the wonder, awe, and love of delight. Pleasure mimics delight but fails to scale the heights of true delight. Pleasure seeks things like meaningless sex, drunkenness, theft, and pride.

I called delight a virtue because I believe it is of ethical and moral concern. If pleasure mimics delight, then delight is the true fulfillment of the things pleasure seeks. The delighted person forsakes meaningless sex for sex only within the covenant relationship of marriage. Husband and wife are supposed to be delighted with one another. The delighted person forsakes drunkenness for true joy. The delighted person is content with their possessions. The delighted person is humble, not thinking too highly of themselves.

Delight is a virtue because it must be intentionally sought. Meaningless sex is easier than lifelong commitment. One night of drunkenness is much simpler than the pursuit of joy. For delight to be a virtue, we must discipline ourselves in it as a runner trains for a marathon or a violinist trains to audition for the orchestra. As the runner and musician carve out time to train and practice, we must carve out time in our lives for the virtue of delight. We Christians call this worship.

In worship, we lift up our heads out of the dreariness of our lives and look to that which is holy, pure, and awesome. In traditional cathedrals, this is modeled for us in the architecture. Our gaze is drawn upwards to the heights of the ceiling, the magnificence of the stained glass windows, to the image of the cross.

In creation, God made things to draw our gaze upward. We are in awe of mountains and their grandeur. We admire the majesty of space and the wonder of the stars. Music and books can draw our eyes metaphorically up and into delight.

My hope is that this volume of stories, poems, and essays draws your gaze upwards toward true delight. Some of the stories or poems meditate on dark themes, but there is hope in even the darkest of times. Hope and delight goes hand in hand. Hope laughs in the face of the things that try and destroy delight. Hope looks at death and pain and contemplates them, but then hope lifts the eyes upward above those things. May you find delight in these pages.

N. K. Carlson, Advent 2019.

POEMS, VOLUME I

ADVENT

By foreign streams we sat in despair
Our hope is dried up like our bones
We are wanderers, vagabonds
Strangers with no home

Our land lies in desolation
Our people are scattered as chaff in the wind
We are waiting for redemption
We are yearning for salvation

We are a people living in darkness
Waiting for a great light
The curtain has gone down on us
But we know it is about to rise

We await a good King
Who will restore our fortunes
We watch through the night
For the hope of dawn

We wait for consolation
Is that a faint gleam on the horizon?
How much longer?
How long, O my soul?

ROUSE THE WATCHMAN

Trees silently wait
The leaves are asleep
With no wind to awaken them from slumber

The waters are still
Smooth and clear as glass
With no wave to disturb the surface

All creation awaits the breath, the wind
Something to stir the stillness
And rouse the watchmen

The musicians are stiff with anticipation
Yearning for resolution
A chord from discord

On top of the lighthouse
He expectantly stares at the horizon
Hoping to behold the ship's return

COMFORT AND DANGER

Absent, and they go unmissed.
Present, a blessing of respite from the scorching radiance of starlight.
Too present,
The very heavens are crashing down on us.
In our midst, and we see nothing but gray glory.
They bring life giving waters and take life in floods.

Good and terrible.
Awesome and awful.
Thunder is the trumpet of God
The foreboding storm is his blanket
Comfort within danger.
Peace within battle.

The ancients saw God in the cloud and they rejoiced and trembled.
His presence provoked love and fear.
He has gathered together the clouds
And hung up his bow,
A mighty hunter home from the field.
He has placed his bow in the sky
To remind us of His mercy and justice.
His rains of grace

And His thunder of judgement
Cumulate in the cumulous.

PASSION

You rode in on a donkey
For everyone to see
Not a king of war
But a king of peace
The people shouted Hosanna
And "blessed is he"
Yet just a few days later
You would hang from a tree

You celebrated Passover
With your friends one last time
One of your friends betrayed you
For a few tiny coins
And after the dinner was over
You left for the garden
And just a few hours later
You would hang from a tree

While in the garden
Anxiously you prayed
Earnestly you asked
"Is there any other way?"
And Judas came and kissed you
And they took you away
And just a few hours later
You would hang from a tree

You stood before Pilate
Who found no fault with you
Yet he handed you over
To the soldiers to kill you
You were whipped and beaten
Cursed and mocked
And just a few minutes later
You would hang from a tree

They nailed your hands
They nailed your feet
A crown of thorns on your brow
Mocking your name
And as you hung in agony
You said it is finished
And you breathed your last breath
Hanging from a tree

Day turned to night
The veil was torn
Your friends they cried
Your mother wept
And those gathered whispered
"He was a righteous man"
And there you were hanging
On that cross for me

Now there was a man named Joseph
A good an upright man
He wrapped your body in cloths
Placed it in a grave
A stone was placed at the entrance
Of the place that you lay
How could you be the messiah,

If you couldn't save yourself?

And then you arose!
As you foretold!
You defeated the grave!
We've been set free
You died in our place
You are the Lord
And now you are
reigning victoriously!

TIS THE SEASON

Tis the season of getting
Tis the season of greed
We give so we can get
And what we don't get we buy

We keep up with the Jones'
Who on earth are they?
We buy bigger and better cars
Nicer and more expensive toys

Tis the season, oh tis the season

Tis the season of excess
Tis the season of self
It begins as soon as we open
Our eyes after our prayer of thanks

Our selfishness knows no bounds
We try to buy the American Dream
But a white picket fence don't mean anything
When the people are dead inside

Tis the season, oh tis the season

Tis the season to move
Tis the season to love
The only way forward for us
Is to the back of the line

SILENCE FALLS

Silence falls, stands up, dusts itself off, and leaves.
Winds of grief bring a blast of ice from the north.
All the light is squeezed out of the sponge that is the world.
The heart aches and the facade breaks the dam of eyes.
Rivers of sorrow flow to the ocean,
Streams of suffering yearn for the sea.
Bleak, black despair rips the joy from the sky,
Depriving us of oxygen,
That which we need to live, move, and be.
Avoid suffering is the refrain,
Though suffering itself produces a void of loss and regret.
Misery's well grows beneath the surface.
Where art thou, O songbird of day?
May silence never fall again.

STRANGE TWINS

Grief invites us to linger in the darkness and despair.
One cannot move on from grief,
for to move on is to deny the part of oneself left behind.
Hospitals, cemeteries, and homes are museums of grief, monuments of memory.
Tombstones watch over the tears of the mourners and the bodies of the broken.
Yet even among the tombstones life moves forward.
Grass grows over the caskets and around the stones marking the places where the dead lie.
Regular cutting, trimming, and mowing are required to restrain the unstoppable force of life.
In the midst of death, life moves forward incessantly.
Pain and sorrow are the garden wence hope springs.
In the dark night of grief, a beam of pure light pierces the sky,
Illuminating not the way on, but the way forward.
In the ocean of chaos, safety lies on the land,
The sturdy footing of hope and peace.
The light shines in the darkness, but the darkness has not understood
How to shine in the light.
Grief and joy are strange twins,
Two sides of the same coin,
Both the price and worth of life.

The ties that bind grief and joy together
Are the tears of the grieving and the tears of the elated.
Grief and joy well up within us until tears spill out of our eyes
To water the dusty ground and bring forth life in abundance.

THORNS

Flower fair, tender bloom, life unstoppable, purity unequaled,
Corrupted by one single animosity and lo, the rose grows thorns.
To prick and injure, not the bearer,
But the one seeking beauty.

Thorns for myself.
Thorns for my children.
Thorns for my grandchildren.
Thorns for my descendants forever.

Those with thorns are left to ponder how it all went wrong.
And so they spend their days outside,
Alone.

The thorns turn inward.
The weapons of wounding wound only the bearer.
Those who live by the thorn die by the thorn.
The flower chokes itself and withers.
Refusing the sun, it resides in utter darkness.

12 YEARS

12 years.
12 years of suffering at the hands of those who claimed to hold the cure.
12 years of spending every last dime on hope, foolish hope to be well.
Well now the collections agency keeps calling.
And calling.
And calling.
12 years.
12 years of being prevented from even the comfort of a touch, a simple touch, let alone an embrace.
And now, hope is gone.
My youth is gone.
My money is gone.
My sanity is gone.
All gone.
Can you see me?

And then...
Life, he came.
He came to town and I thought maybe,
Just maybe,
One touch would do.
One secretive little touch.
No one would know.
The thing I was deprived of for so long will be my salva-

tion.
A touch.
Reaching...
Straining...
Fighting the crowd and reaching...
And there it is.
The touch.
The rough fabric catches on my dry fingers.
And delight courses through my veins.
12 years of misery has been undone by a touch.

SHORT STORIES, VOLUME I

WHEN GOD WEEPS

The Teacher loved my brother, sister, and I,
So when my brother became ill, my sister and I sent for him,
Thinking "he has made the blind see and the lame walk, perhaps he can heal our brother."

The Teacher sent back our messenger and told him to say "This will not end in death, but in glory."

Meanwhile, our brother got worse and worse,
But we took comfort in the promise of the Teacher, who said he would not die.
Every day, I would walk to the edge of the village watching and hoping for the Teacher to appear to heal my brother.

But he never came.
Day after day, he never came.
My brother died.
The Teacher was wrong, and my brother died.
My brother, my only brother is gone.
The Teacher never came.
My brother is gone.
The teacher is a liar.
My brother is
Gone.
Gone.

Gone...

These thoughts and more went through my head.
Hot tears flowed from the eyes of my sister and I.
The anguish and pain of our loss burned a hole in our hearts and the betrayal of the Teacher made it hurt all the more.

Gone.
Gone.
Gone...

On the fourth day after my brother's death,
While we were still in agony, and our friends still were trying to comfort us,
The Teacher came.
He stayed at the edge of the village where I had waited for him.
He asked for my sister and I to come see him.
My sister refused, stung by the fact that he wouldn't come to see us,
So I set off alone.

In the distance, I saw him standing in the middle of the road, a solitary figure.
Seeing him, I ran and buried my face in his chest and let out tears that I thought had dried up due to the greatness of my sorrow.
In between the sobs, I managed to say the thing that was on my heart:
"If you had been here, he wouldn't have died."

Wrapping me tighter in his arms, the teacher said,
"Your brother will rise again.
I am resurrection, I am life.
If you believe in me, even though you die, you will live.

Everyone who lives and believes will never die.
Do you believe?"

"Yes, Teacher."

We entered the village.
When the teacher saw the weeping of my sister and the people, he wept.
Great tears of anguish and pain fell from his eyes as his body shook with tremendous sobs as God wept for his friend.
And those gathered whispered, "See how he loved him."

When he calmed down, he asked to be led to the tomb.
When we arrived, he broke down again.
As he held back tears, he spoke in a loud voice that did not match his wretched state, calling out, "Awake."
His voice was loud and clear and gay, full of life, full of power.

Again, he said "Awake!" this time louder with terrible power and might, like the roar of a lion, it shook the ground.

And again, "Awake."
This time the softest whisper, so soft and gentle, yet everyone heard.
This whisper had even more power in it that the other two.
The word seemed to hang in the air as a bell chimes when struck.
It rang in the air for a fraction of a second or hours, no one knew afterward.

Other than the word, there was no sound.
The wind stopped blowing, the birds stopped chirping, and even the cattle stopped lowing in the solemnness.

All eyes were fixed on the Teacher.
No one moved.

A single tear drop fell from his eye.
It shone like diamond, as if someone had captured light and turned it into liquid.
The tear seemed suspended in the air as it took forever to fall.
With a splash far greater than the small drop should have made,
It hit the ground and shook the earth.

At that instant, a figure appeared at the mouth of the tomb.
My brother stepped into the sun light, alive and well.
He and the Teacher embraced, tremendous, contagious joy radiating from their faces.
Such joy, I had never known.

I believe.

THAT OLD WAR

"...another casualty of that old war," the preacher droned to the crowd assembled on the hillside. It was October, when the leaves were clinging to the trees with such vigor that you would think that winter would never come, but come it must.

"It's always the same thing with these preachers," I said, leaning toward my companion.

He grunted, but said nothing, instead looking down to smooth out the front of his cheap suit. I have an eye for that sort of thing.

The widow is handsomely dressed, all black of course, with a veil that barely covered the side of her face. She wanted to be seen in her grief.

The children too, were smartly dressed. The two boys, neither old enough to shave, were in expensive Italian suits, while their older sister matched her mother almost exactly. There was more grief in her face than the widow's however.

The preacher continued his monologue. "He probably did not even consider if the deceased would like this rubbish," I thought shaking my head.

It was rather warm on this October day, and the sun beat down on the heads of those assembled. I began to have such a marvelous thirst.

"I wish he would hurry it along," I said as I again leaned

over to my companion. He grunted again, clearly agitated at my speaking. No one around seemed to notice my hushed tones.

My mind began to wander as I tried to ignore my growing thirst. We were on the slope of a long, gradually rising hill and I could see another funeral service at the top. There were only two people attending that funeral. There were no seats. The minister and the two mourners formed a triangle around the grave. The minister wore all black. One mourner had dark skin and a long beard, and the other was fair and younger. Several dogs patrolled the perimeter of the triangle. One vaguely resembled one of the mangy strays near my home.

"It's a pity that there is no one there," said I, turning to my companion. "He must have been a nobody."

He glared at me before saying, "There's no such thing as a nobody."

"Oh, you have got to be joking," I said gesturing to the assembled crowd. "Look at all of the assembled for this man! He's a nobody."

"Everybody is a somebody."

Our discussion was interrupted by the crowd standing as one to sing a hymn. I hastened to my feet as the opening line of *Amazing Grace* rose to the heavens. The crowd sang quite poorly, as crowds tend to do. I never cared much for that song.

As the final notes died away, the crowd began to leave. Not too quickly, but slow enough to show some respect. Several went and gave their condolences to the widow. My companion and I stood where we were, watching the crowd. The sun was still beating down on us, and my thirst was quite strong.

"Let us get a drink," I said.

"Wait," my companion said.

"For what?"

"We need to watch the people."

So we did. The crowd dispersed fairly quickly despite their respectful gaits. The widow embraced her children. Only the oldest, the girl, showed any sign of sadness, her sorrow seeming to fall around them like a fog. A breezed picked up, a hot one from the south, and it seemed to take her sorrow with it. The widow and the girl removed their veils and smiled at one another.

"Look at their joy," my companion said.

"I see," said I, as a few leaves blew past our feet. It really was dreadfully hot. I could feel the sweat on my back dripping down.

I looked up again at the other funeral. The three men were each raising a glass. The glasses clinked and then each man drank.

"Let's get a drink," I said again. "Let's go up there and pay our respects, if he really is a somebody."

"We can't."

"What do you mean, 'We can't'?

"You can't get there."

"It's right there. It's a short walk up the hill."

I began walking up the hill, but after a score of paces, the ground seemed to drop away in front of me. There was a chasm that certainly had not been there earlier. At the bottom was a rushing river, nearly a hundred feet below.

"What the H..." I said as I stopped suddenly. My companion had grabbed the back of my coat to keep me from falling.

"Hell is right," my companion said. "Told you you couldn't get over."

"Well damn it all," I said, the thirst now growing ever

stronger in my throat. "All I wanted was some damn water."

"There is no 'damn water,'" said my companion, shaking his head as though this fact were common knowledge and I was ignorant of it.

We looked across the chasm, and the preacher on that side closed his Bible and the two mourners started to wander aimlessly, making toward the chasm, but with no obvious destination in mind.

"Do you recognize them?" my companion asked.

"Of course not," I said, again looking around for a drink. Then I noticed the older of the two men had a water bottle in hand.

"Hey you!" I yelled across, the object of my desire in view. "Toss me that bottle." The man looked up as though surprised to see people across the way. He held up the bottle tentatively.

"It's too far!" he yelled back. He had some sort of accent, maybe middle eastern.

"Throw it, it's not too far!" By now the thirst was excruciating and my voice began to become hoarse.

"I will throw it if you can answer but one question correctly."

"Well let's have it then," I said stamping my foot impatiently.

"What is his name?" he asked, pointing at the younger man beside him.

"Why on earth would I know that?" I said.

"That's right, you didn't know it on earth," he said. "And you don't know it now."

"What do you mean?" said I, stomping my foot.

"This man," the older man said, "was a homeless man on your street for years and years. And you never even looked at him. This man is a son of Abraham. He is my son."

"Well alright, I'm sorry then. I'll make it right."

"You cannot. There is a chasm between you and us."

"Well there must be a bridge or something."

"You have missed the Bridge."

"Now you're just being difficult," I said, furious at his evasiveness.

"Do you not realize what has happened?" the older man said, stroking his beard, sorrow in his eyes. "Two men, two funerals, and a chasm between them. You are dead. That was your funeral down there. This was his funeral up here."

"What? I'm not dead, I'm right here, aren't I?" I turned to my companion. "Tell him I'm not dead."

"I cannot," my companion said.

All of a sudden, the graveyard melted away and the world went dark, as though the sun had gone out. Everything was bathed in firelight. I gripped my companion's arm in fright.

"In your life, you were comforted by your things. And now they are gone and you must deal with the consequences of a life poorly lived."

"Come now, Lazarus," the old man said. "Come to the joy prepared for you." And they walked away into the light on their side of the great divide.

FIRST PATRIOTIC

Glenn and his wife Karen sat down in their usual pew at First Patriotic Church. The service was about to begin. They said hello to those around them as the organist began the prelude, *My Country Tis of Thee*. The organ notes droned through the old sanctuary, reverberating along with walls filled with stained glass depictions of the holiest of saints, the Founding Fathers and the Apostles. High above the altar was a cross set against the backdrop of the American flag. On one side of the cross, carved on what looked to be large tablets of stone, were the Ten Commandments. On the other side, on similar tablets, were the ten articles of the Bill of Rights.

As the final note of freedom rang out, the Reverend stood up. Clothed in a star-spangled robe of navy blue, he lifted his hands to the heavens.

"Brothers and sisters, fellow Americans, I welcome you today in the name of the Father, Son, and Holy Spirit, along with Apostles and Founding Fathers, to First Patriotic Church. We gather together as a Christian nation's Christian church. Let us come before God and before our country and recite the Pledge of Allegiance. If you need the words, they are found in your hymnal on page five."

The congregation stood and pledged allegiance to the flag and the republic. After "liberty and justice for all," the organist began *God Bless America*. At the conclusion of this hymn, the Reverend stood up to preach at the pulpit.

"As you know, today marks the tenth anniversary of the Patriotic Religion Act. In it, our government declared that all religions that do not recognize the glory and majesty of the United States of America are banned. From that monumental day, we at First Patriotic have done our best to make our country a God-fearing one again. We have blended the best of Christianity with patriotism and our faith is stronger than it has ever been. In God we trust and in the United States we trust. Our military has worked hard to make sure that we have the freedom to worship God here today. Let us rise and have a moment of silence for all of our fallen soldiers."

The congregation stood and bowed their heads in reverence. For a minute it was dead silent.

"Almighty Father of our Founding Fathers," the Reverend began praying, "Keep these your United States safe from all enemies and from the workings of the Devil. Allow us the continued freedom in these United States to worship you freely in this promised land. Let all who oppose freedom be like the nations you drove out of the land before your people. Amen."

The congregation remained standing as the organist began another hymn.

Glenn leaned over to Karen and whispered, "I hope he talks more about Jefferson today. That sermon last week about Abraham was so boring."

Karen smiled, but put a finger to her lips to quiet him.

After the hymn, the Reverend began his sermon. To Glenn's delight, he did talk about Jefferson and how the Louisiana purchase was God's work to increase the promised land.

Another hymn followed the sermon and then the Reverend stood up for some announcements.

"If any would join the Lord's Army, we have a sign up table in the atrium where you brave men and women can talk to an Army recruiter. We love our troops and hope that we can send some of our young people to fight God's battles. This Wednesday we continue our study of the Bill of Rights at 7pm in Classroom A. Hope to see you there, unless of course you are at a fair and speedy trial!"

The congregation laughed.

"And lastly, we have an exciting announcement. We are getting a new stained glass window! It will be of Washington crossing the Delaware, Bible in hand, and a cross going up from the boat. It is going to be magnificent. And now, let us stand and sing the National Anthem."

After the anthem, Glenn and Karen filed out of the church. They made lunch plans with the Grahams to go out to eat. On the way, they saw a dozen police cars outside of a house. They were leading out men, women, and children all dressed in their Sunday best.

"Looks like another underground resistance church," Glenn guessed. "Why don't those people admit they're wrong and join our church? We don't bite."

"I don't know, Glenn. They're unpatriotic, that's what they are. All that "Jesus is Lord" and "America is not the Promised Land" stuff is pretty scary. We're a Christian nation. We're the good guys. They're getting what they deserve, those rebels."

And Glenn and Karen continued on their way to lunch, content in their religious fantasy.

DELIGHT IN THE BIBLE

God Delights in Us

In the Bible, delight begins and ends with God. Before we can delight in anything, God takes delight in us. You ever see those street preachers with signs about how everyone is going to Hell and God hates everyone? I doubt they have ever read 2 Samuel 22:20. "He brought me out into a broad place; he rescued me, because he delighted in me."

These are the words of King David. The murderer, rapist, adulterer King David. David was many things including a man of great repentance. When he sinned, he ran back to God and this was what God had in mind when he called him a man after his own heart. God took delight in this very sinful man because that is what God does. God delights in us when we are anything but delightful. God delights in us even though we have sinned against him repeatedly. Why? Because we are his children.

We often talk of how God's grace and mercy are endless, and I think delight belongs in that same category. In creation, God saw the things he had made and they were good. They were delightful. God makes delightful things, including humans.

If you look at what David says, the delight comes

first. "He rescued me, *because* he delighted in me." David needed rescue and God rescued him because he delighted in David. Everything that ever happens with us and God is because he delights in us. It was love and delight that sent Jesus at the first Christmas. It was love and delight that sent him to the cross. Delight has the first and final word in God's dealings with us. When he looks at us, he looks at us with delight because we are his children. He looks at us with delight because we are his special creation. He delights in us and that is good news indeed.

But we are so hard to please. When we find out that God delights in us, we quickly ask the next question: what does God's delight do for us? Numbers gives us a clue. "If the Lord delights in us, he will bring us into this land and give it to us, a land that flows with milk and honey" (Numbers 14:8). This is a classic if-then statement. If God delights in us, then he will bring us into this land. This is an Old Testament promise, but I believe it is one we can lay claim to as Christians. If God delights in us, which we already know is true, then he will bring us into His land, the New Jerusalem spoken of in Revelation. God wants to bring the objects of his delight to himself in a land, a good land, flowing with milk and honey, the best things in creation. God wants to bless those he delights in. We may have to wait for Jesus to come back for this to finally be fulfilled, but we can be confident that God wants what is best for his children. He wants us to live with him.

We Delight in the Lord

In response to God's delight in us, we turn our delight back on our Maker. "Delight yourself in the Lord," Psalm 37 says. Where do we look for our delight? Too often I look to television, books, social media, or something else that is not God. Where does that delight get me? Things we look to for delight that fall short of divine delight will let us down at some point. Rather, we are to delight ourselves in the Lord.

Why though? Why does it matter where our delight is? What about duty and obedience? Sure duty and obedience have their place. Samuel tells King Saul and us, "Does the Lord delight in burnt offerings and sacrifices as much as in obeying the Lord? To obey is better than sacrifice, and to heed is better than the fat of rams" (1 Samuel 15:22). The Lord delights when we obey him, yes, but if we obey simply out of duty, we will soon grow bored of our duty and shirk it. Things done out of duty fail to achieve lofty heights.

Take, for instance, the songwriter. Imagine one songwriter diligently working at his piano each day, playing various melodies, singing, writing down lyrics, all while crafting a song. The problem is, he was assigned this particular song as part of a class on songwriting. He doesn't particularly want to write the song, he does it out of a sense of duty.

Now imagine a second songwriter diligently working at her piano. She plays those same keys, sings a melody, and writes down lyrics. But her motivation is different. She is writing a song because she wants to. Perhaps she is writing it to play for a friend. She works hard, even though the going can be rough because she delights in the journey.

The first songwriter works out of duty, the second out of delight. So it is with our obedience. If we obey from duty, we may be successful in our obedience. This is where legalism slips in unnoticed. Legalism is obedience out of duty with the expectation that others should be similarly dutiful. Obedience from delight his perhaps the most beautiful thing in the world. Obedience from delight says, "I don't think I would do it this way on my own, but I trust you, I delight in you and you delight in me so I will do it your way." If only children would answer their parents this way!

We are to delight ourselves in the Lord because the Lord is delightful. But there is more to this verse. "Delight yourself in the Lord, and he will give you the desires of your heart" (Psalm 37:4). This verse is often treated like a blank check. "Oh," we say, "If I delight in the Lord, he will give me money/a good job/a beautiful wife/a big house/a successful business." That's not how this works at all.

You see, when we delight in God, *He* is the desire of our heart. When we delight in God, he will give us Himself, which really is the best gift anyone could give. Delight begets more delight as the delighted and the object of delight come together. Delight in God, get God. That is the sort of formula that we should be chasing after. God delights in us, and we should delight in him, and when we delight in Him, He gives us Himself.

We Delight in God's Word

Throughout the Bible, there is something else that people are supposed to take delight in. That thing is the word of God. Psalm 1 says it like this: "Blessed is the man... (whose) delight is in the law of the Lord, and on his law he meditates day and night. We are blessed when we delight ourselves in what God has said in his word.

The blessing comes from the meditation. We are to meditate on God's laws, night and day. Does this mean locking ourselves in a closet and simply thinking about scripture 24/7? No. Meditation is more about tasting, savoring, and experiencing. We meditate on God's word by putting it to the test during our daily lives. There is blessing within the living out of God's words and laws.

What does it look like when someone is delighting themselves in God's word and law? "He is like a tree planted by streams of water that yields its fruit in its season, and its leaf does not wither. In all that he does, he prospers" (Psalm 1:3)

The person meditating on God's law is like a tree planted by a stream. The stream provides the needed water for the tree to live and to grow. When we meditate on God's word, we are planting ourselves where we can thrive. God's word provides the nourishment that we need to grow. Without it, we can do no growing. Instead, we wither and die.

When we are planted by the stream, we will bear fruit. The fruit that we bear is love, joy, peace, patience, kindness, goodness, faithfulness, gentleness, and elf-control (Galatians 5:22-23). When we plant ourselves near God's stream, we grow in love. We become more loving and we look more like love. We increase in joy and delight. We have peace near the quiet streams of God.

As a tree follows the course of the seasons, we are patient. We blossom in the spring, grow in summer, lose our leaves in our fall, and lie fallow in winter. And then spring comes again. We learn to be patient in these seasons, waiting on the faithfulness of God to transform us.

By God's stream we grow in goodness and faithfulness. We become more gentle and less violent. We learn to control ourselves. All of this fruit comes from meditation on God's word night and day. When we delight in God, He gives us himself. When we delight in His word, he gives us fruit to bear. His delight in us is the stream that rushes past us, giving us living water to grow and develop into who we were created to be. A mighty tree weathers the storms and seasons. When we grow up in God, we become mighty trees, strong and sturdy, basking in the light of God's delight for us.

SHORT STORIES, VOLUME II

THE MAN WITH NO FACE

While stopped at a red light, I happened to glance in the rearview mirror. To my horror, I saw that the man in the car behind me had no face.

I stared back at him, appalled that where eyes should have been was a blank canvas of skin stretching across his skull. His featureless complexion stared right back, though of course this was silly, men without eyes cannot stare. Still, I had the strangest sensation that he could see, even without eyes. He was driving after all.

Where a nose should have risen above the landscape of his face was a smooth flatness, stretching across the middle of his, well, can I even call it a face? The lack of a mouth was equally unsettling for me. Silent, forever, with no way to speak, this man with no face lacked the portal for communication we all rely on. It looked as though his chin kept going endlessly up into his face.

All of this I took in within the span of a few seconds, before the light turned green and I made my left turn. The man with no face followed me.

At the next red light, I stopped and the faceless man stopped behind me. I again searched his features for any sign of the friendly glint of eyeballs, the familiar shadow of a nose, or the comforting opening of a mouth, but I saw none. The faceless man stared right back at me, and though I knew he could not, he could, in fact, see me. And not just me, but inside of me, to the beating of my heart, the breath inside my lungs, and the electric signals sent to and from my brain. While blind, he saw. While noseless, he could smell. While mute, ever speaking.

"I am the follower. I am the shadow in the dark. I am the breath on your neck when no one is around. I am the movement in the mirror. I am the one who sees your heart, smells your blood, and speaks your name."

As clear as day the man with no face said these things to me as I was stopped at the red light. As soon as it turned green, I drove on, making the first available turn and continuing to drive until I was quite lost myself. At last I came to another red light at a street I recognized.

And there he was, the man with no face, leering at me with the mouthless grin, sniffing the air with no nose, and peering into my soul with those blank stretches of skin which seemed to stretch for miles and miles, swallowing up towns and cities until there was nothing but skin.

Green light, and I was gone. Racing through the streets, trying desperately to somehow get away from the man with no face.

I again made every possible turn, going in no particular direction, my only aim to leave the man with no face far, far behind. And yet...

At the next red light, he was there again. He stared at me, and I stared back at him, through the rearview mirror. And even though the light was red, I stomped on the accelerator and drove through the intersection, narrowly avoiding cars and trucks coming at me from both sides. Horns blared and tires screeched, and somehow I was through the intersection, safe.

And then I heard a loud crash, and I looked back so see the car the man with no face was driving come to a halt after being t-boned by another car. By now I was too far away to see the man with no face, but I kept going, triumphant in my escape.

I made it home in good time, with the good fortune of only experiencing green lights.

The doorbell rang at ten o'clock that evening. I paused the television and walked to the door, flipping on the porch light. I opened to door to reveal the man with no face. He was more horrible in person than it had been in my rearview mirror. He stood there, illuminated against the black night. His cheek, if we can call it that, had a scrape, presumably from the accident. His face radiated rage. With no facial features at all, this is hard to explain, but it seemed that every cell of his abominable face was united in one singular pursuit: my destruction.

Face to face with something out of a nightmare, I was speechless, frozen in place. For hours, it seemed, we stared at each other through the glass door, my nightmare and I. In utter revulsion, I finally pulled myself together and shut the door and bolted it. I heard the glass door swing open, and he knocked thrice.

"Go away, go away you fiend," I yelled through the door, holding it shut with the weight of my body.

He knocked again, harder, louder. Somehow the sound of knocking pierced my chest and I doubled over in pain. It was utter agony, as though a void had opened up where my heart had been, a black hole sucking in everything around it.

"Leave me alone!" I screeched through gritted teeth as the pain began to travel from my chest to my neck. I sank to my knees, clutching at my chest and neck.

The man with no face knocked a third time, softly this time. Tap, tap, tap.

I could get no words out as the pain went from my neck to my face. My whole body went limp and everything went dark as I crashed to the floor.

Hours later, in the light of morning, I came to myself and I found that I was lying on the ground just inside my front door. I stood up and opened the door to see if the man with no face had gone.

There stood a man with a face. He stood there looking at me, blinking in the sunlight. He cocked his head to the side, studying me. He looked familiar. His eyes resembled my mother's.

"Who are you?" is what I meant to ask.

But no words came out. The words caught in my throat and a low grunting was the only sound. The man with eyes like my mother's smiled at me, a wicked, evil grin. His smile filled me with more foreboding than I had yet felt in these strange hours since the beginning of this tale. Then he turned and walked away, disappearing down the street. I went to the bathroom to wash my face. I turned on the tap and splashed some water against my smooth face. I dried off with the towel and then I glanced up into the mirror and the man with no face stared back at me.

THE BATTLE OF MIDTOWN MALL

It was a cold and dreary Black Friday morning and the mall was already packed with people. Stephanie walked out of a store with her bags on her arm, pushing the receipt into her purse. She was agitated.

"I can't believe they are out of that shirt I wanted," she complained to her friend, Amy. "They were picked clean. And it's only eight in the morning!"

"There seem to be more people here than usual," Amy said as a haggard looking man rushed past, clutching what appeared to be the entire contents of the nearby toy store.

"Humph," Stephanie grunted, looking over the heads of the crowd to scope out their next shop. "I wish they'd all stay home."

"The deals are too good," Amy said, shaking her head.

The two women walked down the crowded concourse, bumped every so often by someone in a hurry. They were both getting frustrated.

They arrived at one of the huge anchor stores, ready to find the deals they craved.

"God, I live for this," Amy said, inhaling deeply through her nose as if the aroma of deals was a thing to be smelled.

They walked in and began looking at shirts and dresses.

"Oh, I like this one," Stephanie said, holding up an elegant blue ball gown. "This would be perfect for that Christmas gala."

"You should get it," Amy said.

"It's $300 dollars, and that's on sale," Stephanie said sadly. "Oh, and it's the last one in my size. I'll think about it."

Amy knew that was code for, "I really want it but I can't afford it."

Another woman picked up the dress that Stephanie was just looking at, checked the price tag, and put it back on the rack, shaking her head.

Stephanie and Amy continued to shop around, each accumulating a dozen or so pieces to try on in the fitting room.

Then three beeps rang out from seemingly everywhere. "Attention shoppers. All items purchased in the next ten minutes will be an additional 15% off. Thank you."

For a split second, it was the calm before the storm. Then all hell broke loose. Shoppers burst into action, some rushing to the register, some rushing to pick up items previously too expensive.

"I'll get in line and save us a spot," Amy yelled over the commotion.

"I'm going to get that dress!" Stephanie yelled back.

Amy pushed toward the register and Stephanie went against the tide toward that glorious, blue dress. She pushed past a mom and her two kids, and didn't even glance back to say sorry. She herself was nearly toppled over by an overzealous woman with a mountain of blue jeans in her arms.

"Hey! Watch where you're going!" she shouted at the back of the woman. Then she continued to press forward toward her prize.

She got in reach and lunged, grasping the dress by the shoulder. At the exact same instant, the other woman who had looked at the dress grasped the other shoulder. Both women paused for a moment and looked into each other's eyes. Then like lionesses, they started yelling.

"I was here first!" the other woman yelled, trying to pull the dress from Stephanie's hand.

"Yeah right," Stephanie yelled back. "I saw you look at it after me!"

"How dare you!" the other woman screamed, dropping her other things to take a two-handed approach at securing the dress.

"Oh no you don't!" Stephanie yelled. With one hand firmly on the dress, she used her other to push over the rack the dress was on, directly into the woman's side. She went down in a fabulous dress avalanche.

"Ha!" Stephanie yelled, victoriously. She took off toward the register. She spied Amy and began making her way over there when she was tackled from behind. The other woman had freed herself from the dress pile and made a beeline toward Stephanie. Stephanie's purchases and other items fell to the floor and the two women rolled around on the floor, each trying to win the dress. Several other shoppers tried to intervene, but it was no use. They rolled into the nearby power tools section.

A man jumped in, and tried to separate the two, but he was quickly beaten back by a nails and teeth. If that weren't bad enough, he was soundly punched in the face by another man.

"That's my wife," the second man, who must have been the husband of the other woman, said as he punched the first man. The first man fell to the floor, but quickly jumped up and tackled the second man. Other shoppers, both men and women joined the fray, initially trying to stop the fight, but quickly drawn into their own altercations with other would be peacekeepers.

A mall cop rode up on his Segway, blowing his whistle and yelling. His words and whistle did no good.

Merchandise stands went everywhere as dozens of people clashed in the Battle of Midtown Mall as it later came to be known.

"To me, to me, you shoppers who want peace and will not yield to the forces of darkness!" yelled one man, who was setting up a fortified position using fallen merchandise racks. "To me, you warriors of peace!" About half of the mob fell back into the fortified position, including Stephanie.

"To me, to me, all who have been wounded and oppressed by these miscreants!" a woman called out, and Stephanie was surprised to see her original opponent mustering her troops to storm the fortified position. The mall cop continued to blow his whistle.

From the fortified position, Stephanie and her company began lobbing anything they could at the approaching army. Hangers, drills, beaded necklaces, all were tossed at the advancing hoard.

"We can't hold them off forever," Stephanie screamed as she hurled a hanger into the face of an opposing soldier.

She was right. Already the walls were being breached by the intruders and her comrades were falling left and right.

And then three beeps sounded again and Amy's voice came over the intercom.

"We fight for freedom!" she yelled, and Stephanie looked around to see where she was. Amy was sitting on the shoulders of a huge man near the customer service station. Many other women were similarly position on the shoulders of men. "Charge!" she yelled into the speaker before dropping it. She had in her hand a long metal pole used for retrieving clothing from high shelves. Her army charged into the invading throng, flanking them from the back. Her pole gleamed as she drove into the enemy. The cavalry had arrived to rescue the defenders!

After several minutes of intense fighting, the remaining attackers had surrendered and Stephanie and Amy hugged.

"I thought I'd never see you again," Stephanie said, a tear in her eye, which she wiped away with a blood-stained hand. "Thank you for saving us."

"It was my pleasure," Amy said, grinning. "Now let's get you that blue dress."

THE WOMAN IN THE ROOM

As I sat in my chair reading, a woman entered the room in her nightgown. She silently glided across the room and lay down in bed. It gave me such a fright.

"What are you doing in my room?" I asked her, puzzled and afraid. But she took no notice of me.

I must be dreaming, I thought to myself. I made my way from the room and sat down on the couch in the living room. *I'll wake up shortly.*

I must have dozed off on the couch. I retrieved my book from the floor where it had fallen. I was surprised that the noise of it falling had no woken me.

The bed was perfectly empty and the bed was made. Convinced that I had dreamed the whole thing, I set about my day.

That evening again, I found myself in my chair in the room, reading my book. Again, the woman walked in, clad in her nightgown. She saw me and screamed. The scream echoed in that room off of the wood floor and reverberated in a spooky manner.

I stood up.

"I don't know why you are, or why you are here, but please leave," I said as sternly as I could but my voice quivered and shook.

She wordlessly and silently glided backward from the room, not taking her eyes off me. When she was gone, I let out my breath which I had not known I was holding. After a few minutes, I walked into the hallway and through the house. There was no trace of the woman.

Some sort of ghost, I thought to myself, shaking my head. I resolved to get more sleep.

I must have fallen asleep in my chair, for the next thing I knew, the woman was back, clothed in normal clothes. With her was a priest.

I quickly stood up, "You must leave!" I exclaimed, unable to find other words.

The priest nodded and pulled out a crucifix. "In the name of the Father, and the Son, and the Holy Spirit, be gone from here you spirit."

"What are you talking about?" I asked, taking a step forward. The woman stepped back and the priest spread his arms wide as though to shield her.

"This is not where you belong," he bellowed at me. By now I was utterly bewildered. Was a ghost priest exorcising me from my own house?

"This is my home!" I yelled back, thinking I was going mad at the absurdity. "This is my room. This is my bed. This is my chair!" I gestured at the chair.

"This is my house!" the woman yelled, getting her courage and stepping forward, next to the priest. "Look!"

I looked around the room with fresh eyes. The bed and chair were familiar. On the nightstand was a clock, a book, and a picture. I moved forward to look at the picture, and the priest stepped back in front of the woman. I ignored them and kept moving. The woman was in the picture, smiling with another woman, perhaps her sister.

"What the..." I said, perplexed. "How...?"

"Do you see now?" the priest said. "This is not your place. It's time to move on."

I tried to pick up the picture but my hand when right through the frame. I looked at my hand and could see through it to the floor below. At last I knew.

"I am so very sorry," I said, looking to the woman. "I did not know."

"Be gone, friend. Move on," the priest said.

"I shall. I shall go on. At last I know the truth. I shall go on."

And with that, I swept through the room, through the wall into the hallway. I had been using doors and such as a ghost for so long. How silly of me.

FAMILY SECRET

Wendy was taking a few moments to straighten up in the playroom while the twins, Cassidy and Jake, took their nap. Somehow their toys were everywhere, despite only playing in there for a few minutes.

After picking up the toys, she walked down the hall toward the kitchen, intent on preparing lunch. Halfway down the hall, she stopped. Mr. Edwards' home office door was ajar. She had never seen this door open, and in her two years of nannying for the Edwards, she had never even known it to be unlocked. She looked back and forth down the hallway, even though she knew no one to be there. Mr. and Mrs. Edwards would not be home for several hours.

She knew she should stay out, but her curiosity got the better of her. She gently pushed the door open, peering around it. She was slightly disappointed to see a normal looking office. But as she thought about it for a moment, she did not know what she expected. Bookshelves held books on law and business. The large, wooden desk stood in the center of the room, a high backed leather chair behind it. There were filing cabinets along the wall behind the desk, below the window. Wendy was just about to leave when she noticed the closet door slightly ajar. She knew that she should just back out and close the door, but her curiosity got the better of her. She walked across the room, tiptoeing to avoid making nose, but the large rug cushioned her steps, so it was unnecessary. She gently opened the closet door and found several suits hanging up. On the floor were some dress shoes and a small safe. The safe was locked, of course.

Stepping out of the closet, Wendy stepped over to the desk. The leather chair looked so comfortable so she sat down in it. She put her hands on the desk and felt strangely powerful, until she knocked a pen off of the desk and onto the floor. She was so frantic that she accidentally kicked the pen further under the desk. She hastily got down on hands and knees and retrieved it. While she was down there, she noticed a nail sticking out of the wood in the corner of the desk and on that nail there hung a small sliver key. She paused, contemplating the situation. She knew that the key probably went to the lock box.

Her curiosity again got the better of her. She grabbed the key and seconds later found herself sliding it into the lock on the safe. It clicked and the door swung open. The only thing inside was a large envelope, which of course Wendy reached for and opened. In it were several pictures. She recognized the two Edwards children, Cassidy and Jake, in all of them, but she did not recognize the two other people, a man and a woman who appeared in the pictures. The twins appeared to be a year old. Looking closer, she noticed that the pictures were taken from outside of whatever house the four subjects were in.

Wendy's mind started racing. What did this mean? Who were the man and woman? Why did Mr. Edwards have these pictures of them?

She heard a noise in the hallway and hastily stuffed the pictures back in the envelope and the envelope into the safe, which she locked. She practically threw herself under the desk to hang up the key and flew across the room back into the hallway, pulling the door shut behind her. Her heart was beating so fast.

The noise she heard was one of the twins on the baby monitor, but it had sounded like footsteps. She breathed a sigh of relief and went to check on the twins. Jake was up, so she grabbed him and took him to the kitchen, where she sat him down at the table while she made him a snack. He kept up a steady stream of monologue, but she was not really paying attention. She was thinking about what she had seen.

The rest of the day, her mind wandered to the pictures of the twins and some unknown people. Were those the real parents? She didn't know what to think. When Mr. and Mrs. Edwards arrived home, she hastily bid them farewell and drove quickly down the block. Her heart was pounding.

That night as she was trying to fall asleep, a bolt of fear went straight through her heart. *What if Mr. Edwards found evidence that she had been in his office?* She was pretty sure that she hadn't left anything behind or left and evidence of her ever being there. *There's fingerprints,* she thought to herself, going cold with dread. The rational part of her mind knew that Mr. Edwards didn't dust for fingerprints in his office, especially with no reason to suspect anyone had been there. But the fearful part of her mind kept shouting down the rational part. She tossed and turned all night, fearing her dismissal as nanny, or something much worse.

In the morning, Wendy drove to the Edwards home, looking as tired as she felt. She felt like she was driving to her own funeral.

When she entered the front door, the twins came running and screaming in delight toward her. She hugged them both and hung her coat up in the hall closet. Mr. and

Mrs. Edwards were finishing up breakfast in the kitchen.

"Good morning, Wendy," Mrs. Edwards said cheerfully. "There's coffee in the pot."

Whew, Wendy thought to herself. *They don't know.* Within ten minutes of her arrival, both Mr. and Mrs. Edwards said goodbye to her and the twins and left for work. Wendy resolved to not let her curiosity get the better of her.

She had a normal morning of running around with three-year-olds. She took them to the park to enjoy the fall air. After the park, they had lunch and then went down for their nap. She collapsed on the couch in the living room, exhausted from her duties and from not sleeping a wink the night before. She grabbed the remote and turned the TV to a soap opera that she occasionally watched when she had a spare moment. The characters were engaged in some sort of romantic drama.

Wendy looked up at the clock above the TV to check how long the twins had been down when her eyes were drawn to the picture frames on the mantel. She stood up and walked over, looking at each picture. They were normal family photos. Group shots of the whole Edwards family, individual shots of each twin, and a couple of the twins together. None of the pictures showed the twins to be younger than a year old. *Were there any baby pictures in the house?*

Her curiosity was now fully roused and she quietly crept around the house, partly to avoid waking the twins and partly because she knew she was snooping. Like most families with small children, the Edwards kept pictures of the twins all over the house. There were pictures hanging in hallways, pictures on shelves in the dining room, even pictures scrolling on the smart screen in the kitchen. Yet

Wendy saw no baby pictures. She decided to try the office door again, but it was locked today.

That night, she decided to do more research into Mr. and Mrs. Edwards. She found their biographies on their company websites. She saw that they had moved from Seattle just before she began nannying for them. She knew that already because they told her. But now it was clue.

She typed "missing children Seattle 2017" into Google. The results were databases of missing persons on Washington. She scrolled down the page and a result from the *Tacoma Times* caught her attention.

"Parents Go Missing on Hike." She read the article, about how a man and a woman, Eric and Maddy Peterson, mysteriously went missing on a hike in the mountains. The twins were a year old. The article included a picture of the couple. Wendy could not be sure if they were the people in the pictures she had seen in Mr. Edwards' office. If only she had made copies or taken a picture of them!

Wendy clicked over to Facebook and looked up Eric Peterson and then Maddy Peterson. There were a million people by those names, but she could not find any in Washington. Maybe they hadn't had Facebook. She checked Twitter and Instagram but again could find no trace of the people she was looking for. *They either didn't have social media or someone tried really hard to hide any trace of them.*

For the next few days, her mind dwelled on the missing Petersons and their two children. She needed to get into Mr. Edwards office again to look at those pictures to see if the people in them were the Petersons.

She hatched her plan. The door knob had a simple lock on it. She knew that because she found herself studying it when she walked back. She searched online about how to get into a room in a house if you locked yourself out. She found that a straightened out paperclip could slide in the lock and trigger the mechanism, opening the door.

Mr. Edwards carefully locked the door every time he used the room, so she carefully planned the day and time of her attempted break in. Mr. Edwards was going on a business trip soon and Wendy felt better about attempting to break into his office when he was out of the state. She would do it during the twins' nap time.

The night before, she called her friend Emily.

"Emily, I need to tell you something and you're going to think it's silly, but you have to take me seriously."

"Of course, Wendy, what's up?" Emily asked.

"I think the family I nanny for might not have gotten their children legally."

"What?" Emily asked, incredulously.

Wendy told Emily about the office and the pictures and about discovering the Petersons online.

"I don't really know what to think, but I have a weird feeling that Cassidy and Jake are those two twins from Washington!"

"Wendy," Emily began, choosing her words carefully. "Don't you think you're reading into this too much? When I met them, Mr. and Mrs. Edwards seemed like nice people."

"I know what I saw," Wendy said stubbornly. "Those pictures were taken from outside of the house. What kind of person takes pictures like that?"

"It's a shame you don't have the pictures still," Emily said.

"I'm going to try to get in there and see them again. And I'll take pictures this time," Wendy said.

"Wendy, you're going to get yourself fired!" Emily exclaimed. "Or worse," she added in a low voice.

"I have to find the truth. I'm in too deep."

"Well now you just sound like you're in a movie."

"Emily, be serious! I am going back in to the office tomorrow. I will get to the bottom of this."

Wendy finished filling Emily in on the rest of the plan.

"Sounds risky, Wendy," Emily said.

"I have to risk it."

***

At 2 o'clock the next afternoon, Wendy put the twins down in their beds for a nap. She paced up and down the hallway, hesitating. She brought gloves today. It just felt right. She kept pacing but could not bring herself to open the door. Then she thought about the Petersons. If there was even the slightest chance that Cassidy and Jake were their kids, she had to find the truth. If she was wrong, things could continue on as they had been for two years. If she was right...

She knelt at the door and inserted the paperclip into the lock. She wiggled it around until she felt the mechanism and pushed in. The door handle turned easily and the door swung open gently. *No going back now,* she thought to herself.

She walked cautiously into the room, still afraid of Mr. Edwards, even though she knew he was hours away. The desk was neat and tidy. She walked around behind it and dropped to her knees, crawling under to find the key. It was not there.

And then the door shut. Wendy's blood went cold and every hair on her neck and arms stood straight up.

"I think you are looking for this," a voice said. Wendy stood up slowly and saw Mrs. Edwards twirling the safe key on her left index finger. In her right hand was a pistol pointing straight at Wendy. She stood in front of the door.

"You don't look happy to see me," she said, smiling a cold, joyless smile at her nanny.

"Mrs. Edwards, I can explain," Wendy said, her voice an octave higher than normal.

"There is nothing to explain, Wendy," Mrs. Edwards said. "You know they say curiosity killed the cat."

"I... I..." Wendy stammered, but she could not think of anything else to say.

"Save it," Mrs. Edwards said. "Do sit down, please," she said, gesturing to the leather chair with her gun. Wendy sat down.

"Good. Now, to business." Mrs. Edwards paced in front of the door. "We knew you had been here. My idiot husband left the door unlocked. When he got home that night, he noticed that something didn't feel right in here and checked on the safe. He noticed the pictures had been touched. But what to do about it?"

Wendy mentally calculated what it would take to tackle the woman and take her gun.

"We figured you would try to get in here again, if you were as curious as we thought. I volunteered to stay home these past few days and wait here in case you showed up again. If you didn't come in here again, we wouldn't need to deal with any of this unpleasantness," she said, looking at her gun. "You had no proof of anything so you were not a threat."

"So you are hiding something."

"Of course, I'm glad you worked that out. If we didn't have a secret do you think I would be standing here with a gun? I waited at desk quietly each day. I heard you try the knob a few times. I would hide in the closet until I knew you had moved on. I barely made it today as you were fidgeting with the lock."

"Are the twins yours?" Wendy asked, still analyzing what it would take to leave this room alive. For the time being, she would keep Mrs. Edwards talking.

"Finders keepers," Mrs. Edwards said coldly.

"Did you kill those people?"

Mrs. Edwards rolled her eyes. "What do you think? What do you deduce?"

"You murdered the Petersons and took their kids and moved here."

"So close, but so, so far away, dear. You'll have to do better than that."

"So tell me then."

"Well, for one, we are not murderers. Call us killers if you like, or executioners, but we are not murderers."

"You killed them, that makes you murders."

"No, no, no, we did not kill them just to kill them. It was their punishment for what they did to me."

Now Wendy was very confused. "What did they do to you?"

Mrs. Edwards rubbed the back of her right hand against her forehead in a dramatic manner, made all the more dramatic by the gun still clutched in that hand. She pulled a seat close to Wendy and sat down, leaning forward, gun pointing again at her captive.

"They stole everything from me," Mrs. Edwards said, her voice low and menacing. Wendy waited, hoping that Mrs. Edwards would tell the story and get distracted enough to be overpowered.

"The Petersons were our friends. We all owned a business together. But then we discovered that Eric was stealing from the company. We confronted him. He and my husband got into an altercation. In the fight, Eric lashed out and kicked me in the stomach. I was pregnant." Her eyes looked as though she was staring miles away and years into the past.

"Our baby didn't survive. I miscarried. It was a girl. We kicked the Petersons out of the business, but the damage was already done. They baby was gone, the money was nearly gone, and we had lost our friends. The police didn't do anything. They just kept saying they would look into it, but nothing ever came of it. So we took matters into our own hands. We watched the house. We found they were going on vacation to the mountains. We followed them. We pushed them into a river near a waterfall. Their bodies were swept away. We returned to their house and picked up the twins. Two precious children to replace ours. We moved here and started over."

Wendy didn't know what to say, but she knew the moment for her desperate bid for freedom was coming soon. She looked at the clock on the wall. Outside, the wind blew and the house creaked.

"So now what to do with you?" Mrs. Edwards asked. "You know too much now. That's what I get for blabbing." She rubbed her forehead with the back of her hand again.

As Mrs. Edwards brought her hand back down, several things happened simultaneously. Wendy kicked up at the gun in Mrs. Edwards' hand, which went off, blasting a hole in the ceiling. The gun fell to the floor. The door to the office was violently kicked in and several police officers ran in, guns drawn. Mrs. Edwards fell back in surprise and landed on her back. Wendy finished her kick and stood to her feet, ready to fight. Adrenaline pulsed through her veins and she felt like she could push over a truck.

Two of the police officers pulled Mrs. Edwards to her

feet and cuffed her. They read her Miranda Rights.

"Are you alright?" one of the officers asked Wendy. "We got a call that there might be trouble here."

"I am so glad you are here. I have got a story to tell you." Wendy pulled out her phone and pushed stop on the recording app. "They took the babies. They killed the parents. Here, she said everything. It's all here," Wendy said, handing him the phone. "Make sure you arrest her husband, too."

From the other side of the house, they began to hear the sounds of crying children.

"Can I go check on them?" Wendy asked. "I'm the nanny."

"Leave the phone here and I will listen to what it says, but yes, go check on the children."

Wendy left the room and gently opened the door to the twins' room.

"I don't know what is going to happen to you," she told the twins as she bounced them on her knees. "But I do know that I will always be watching over you."

The twins snuggled up to their nanny, oblivious to anything other than her voice and touch.

THE SECRET OF CREATIVITY

When the creativity strikes, we can write all the books, paint all the paintings, and write all the songs.

Sadly, it feels like we are only ever inspired part of the time. How can we find inspiration when inspiration feels like trying to catch smoke in a hand?

It Starts With Delight

The secret of fostering creativity is delight. Delight means looking at the world as a wonderful place, full of possibilities and adventure. Being a person of delight means finding joy and pleasure in the world.

Our English word comes from the Latin word *delectare, which means* "to charm." When we are delighted, we are charmed by the wonder of the world. Delight pulls us into its spell.

Delight is the spark of creativity. A delighted artist creates something delightful. Delightful creations have the power to charm readers, watchers, and viewers and pull them into the delightful story the artist is telling with words, song, or paint.

Even in laments, delight is there in the shadows. Delight is the hope that the world can be wonderful even if it is not right now.

Practicing Delight

Delight is not something that happens to us but something in which we participate. A small child laughing with delight at leaves falling from the trees demands a response. We can ignore the delight before our eyes or we can join in and be delighted alongside the child.

Delight is a discipline that must be sought. Children find delight so much easier to experience than adults. Somewhere along the line, we have bought into the lie that we must restrain our emotions, even our good emotions like wonder, joy, and delight. When we restrain delight, we live shadow lives, half of who we truly are.

If you are in a creative rut, seek delight. Take a walk in nature. Watch the trees, the grass, and the animals. Look at the reflection of the sky in the water. Find instances of delight in nature. Go to a park and watch the children laugh. Look at a mother delighting in her child. Visit a museum and experience the wonders inside. Walk into a cathedral and marvel at the grand architecture which points one's gaze upwards.

C. S. Lewis said, "We are half-hearted creatures, fooling about with drink and sex and ambition when infinite joy is offered us, like an ignorant child who wants to go on making mud pies in a slum because he cannot imagine what is meant by the offer of a holiday at the sea. We are far too easily pleased."

We settle for imitations of delight when the real thing is there to behold and to be experienced. We pretend to be under a spell when the real charm of delight is there waiting to be grasped.

If you are a creative, seek delight while it may be found. It's the small moments where we live as we were made to live, even for just a second.

POEMS, VOLUME II

FIND ME IN THE NORMAL MAGIC

Find me in the normal magic of a summer's day
When the children laugh, and run, and play
Walking by faith and not by sight
Means journeying in the world of delight

Consider the tree, majestic and tall
Its leaves turn orange and fall
Its roots dig deep in the dark, warm earth
A living statue of drawn out mirth

Or look to the flowers which are here for today
Yet when winter comes they all go away
Each precious shoot with colors galore
All joining together and adding to more

Maybe I could tempt you to gaze on the waters
In the waves play, our sons and our daughters
The way the light reflects on the rivers and streams
Help us appreciate the sun's warm beams

Lastly would you look to that far off cave
The one that they used as his burial grave
But in one moment dawn came from night
And death could not hold him, he is our delight

YEARNING BESIDE THE CHERRY TREE

Yearning beside the cherry tree one is cherishing the sweet smell of summer breeze perpetually when one is young and in love.

In fascination and infatuated with passion beyond the rational satisfaction that comes when one is young and in love.

The heart wants what the heart wants and the hearth glows white hot with the fire, embers, and what not when one is young and in love.

Enchanted by the advancement of can't stop feeling for the beloved, heart chanting and hands sweating when one is young and in love.

Drink from the well of love's inebriation returning and sipping each day with no hesitation when one is young and in love.

OF TIDE AND BILLOW

relentless
flow of continuous
explosions of brine
making up for lost time
and gathering back
together as
troops
rest before the
bitter charge into battle
wave after wave of cavalry
beats back the enemy
of time and earth
regrouping
in the offing
collected
for the time
being timeless, infinite
eternity told by the clock
of tide and billow
the ticking by
which the
Watchmaker
Breathes

DAYTIME STARLIGHT

Daytime starlight falls as snow from heaven above.
It heaps on cars and streets,
The brilliance and the heat
Rise to form a canopy of delight.

Oh moderation, the glare strikes my eyes,
Dazzling and blinding,
As radiation flows through the streets
Like a river of luminous prayer
In the garden of the Lord.

Run, you darkness, flee before your doom.
All will be illuminated,
All shadows will be conquered
You made your home in holes and caves
And now your shelters are laid bare before the sun.
You are vanquished by the light.

Sons of Adam, daughters of Eve,
Step out into the light.
Come, be not afraid.
For though the sun scorches
The hand of the almighty is your shade.

He is a mighty tree,
Protecting those who take refuge in him.
He will hide you in himself,
In the light as He is light incarnate.

Oh sunshine, oh Son shine on us.

FOR THE WRITERS

In the beginning,
You created the world.
Every mountain, every valley,
A fictional paradise.

And it was good.

With that knowledge, rest well.
You are a creator.
You did the thing.
Blank paper blossoming with life.
And characters.
Backstories galore.

And you did well.

So on the late nights
When you are banging your head on your desk in frustration
Because the creativity just won't come anymore,
Remember that from you flows a deep well setting, plot, and characters,
People. Places. Things.
Created out of nothing
Like magic.

Brew that coffee extra strong.

You're going to need that liquid strength
To keep going.
Let the aroma wash over you,
Invigorating your mind and soul.

Don't give up,
Don't ever give up.
You have got this.
You are a creator
And creators create.

You are more than your word count.
You are more than your income.
You are a writer.

So here's to you,
You creators of worlds,
You makers of people,
You crafters of story,
You wordsmiths,
You writers.
Don't give up.
Don't ever give up.
Keep writing.
One word at a time.
Write.
Now.

ABUNDANCE

You looked into the dark and imagined the universe
You spoke the word and it was so
Every galaxy and every atom proclaiming
That you're the God of Abundance

Oh God give us Heaven's dew
And the richness of the world
An abundance of food and drink

We thank you for your bread and your wine
The richness of your body and blood
Broken and poured out in abundance for us

You planted a garden and raised it up in love
You gave it into our care
Every blade of grass and every tall tree proclaims
That you're the God of Abundance

Oh God give us more of you
And the riches of your grace
An abundance of hope and joy

We thank you for your bread and your wine
The richness of your body and blood
Broken and poured out in abundance for us

We may walk through fire and water
But you are bringing us to a land of abundance

The darkest valley seeks to consume us
But you bring us to your promised land

Oh God give us mercy new
And the embrace of the cross
An abundance of sorrow and love

We thank you for your bread and your wine
The richness of your body and blood
Broken and poured out in abundance for us

SUGAR MAPLE

By the river we sat and we sang
In the shadow of the sugar maple tree.
Songs of life and love and loss
Drift upward in the wind through the branches and leaves
Grandfather planted this tree on the bank of the stream
“Be like this tree,” he said,
“Plant yourself by a lifesource.
Dig down.
Be rooted.
Be present.”

We grew up with the tree, though not as high.
It was our older brother and our younger sister.
Silent. Present.

In its shade we played and imagined that I was our fortress.
By its roots we buried memories and loss.

May its leaves never wither and its shade never cease,
As long as the seasons change.
So may we be.

MOUNTAINS RISE

Over the plains the mountains rise
Towers of majesty and awe
The wonders of them reach the skies
Aloft with nature's splendor, unrefined and raw

Next to the path a river runs swift
Water from the mountains battlement
One more of the Maker's many gifts
This stream gives drink and refreshment

The song of the world is a song of old
A song of love and loss and more
A tune from when the world was new and cold
A melody of yearning for distant shore
Snow graces those lofty peaks
A reminder of the hardships above
But in the mountains we can seek
The One who made the peaks in love

DREAMS

We are all storytellers at night
Our minds compose tales of wonder and woe
Fantasy and failure

Everything is possible
And yet, nothing is probable.

Our mental pictures rival
The motion pictures
When it comes to plot twists and turns

But when we are in the brightness of the day
Crystal clear yet our minds cloudy
We are unable to tap into our abilities as yarn weavers
Tale spinners
Legend makers
We exist, but only just
Our day dreams are cheap imitations of the delights
Which our minds craft while we are asleep

WORDS

One
At
A
Time
As we
Grow older
Stronger, wiser
Learning to harness
The power of
Speech and words
To get our way
To communicate our needs
To encourage others and tear down
The avalanche grows larger and larger
As the successive weight of words collects
Into a roaring monster that cannot be stopped
Until we learn to subdue the rudder steering the ship
And then instead of being controlled we control the tide of words
Shaping them and wielding them for joy and delight.

WISHES

Imagine the future
And all the possibilities of what could be,
What should be,
What will be.
Reach down and grasp the brush of hope
And paint the future with strokes of love, laughter, and delight.
Make markings of yearning
Use all the colors of longing
All our wishes
All our dreams
Exist for one shining moment of expectation
And infinite possibility
In the minds of dreamers and creators
Now, pick up your tool
Be it brush, pen, or song,
And work to make that glorious future a reality
Dream the future and get it down in blueprints and chord charts
And bring that future to life.

WINTER MEETS ITS DEATH

The bleak season of death transforms into new creation,
A yearly resurrection woven into the fabric of time and nature.
The world begins again, gray to green,
Barren wasteland to fertile wonderland.
Gardens spring to life as the Word sprang to life in a garden.
All things are made new.
Winter cannot win, the Lion always comes,
And winter meets its death.

THE THINGS THAT CHARM US

Magic has a hold on us. Whether it is the Deep Magic from the dawn of time or the Deeper Magic before the dawn of time in Narnia, the magic found in Harry Potter, or the Force in Star Wars, we are always looking to magic.

Unfortunately for us, magic is fleeting in our world. We cannot walk into Olivander's to get a wand. We are not familiar with the Force. But that doesn't mean that we are consigned to a magic-less existence.

In the very fabric of the world, God has woven magic. This magic is indeed deeper magic from before the dawn of time. This magic is found within the Trinity. This magic is delight.

Delight is from a Latin word which means "to charm." Delight is something that charms us. This charm is found within God's good creation.

I specifically want to talk about three things that charm us. These three things all have a hold over us in a way that is similar to a magic spell. I believe that God made all three of these things to charm us.

The Magic of Music

The first thing that charms us is music. This is perhaps the very first thing we experience from within our mother's womb as she sings over us. The sound waves which form melody and rhythm reach our ears before we are even born. The sound of a mother singing charms the child within her.

Music continues to charm for the rest of our lives. Children learn things about our world through song. Music is connected with our memory. It's magical. I believe God wired us this way for a reason.

As we grow older, we become emotionally attached to a melody. There is a reason that movies include a score. The music compliments the visual images to create an emotional experience. Music can convey happiness, sadness, anger, frustration, completeness, conflict, resolution, and a host of other things. Think of the music of Star Wars or Lord of the Rings. These songs create emotions within us with no words or visuals whatsoever. That's magic right there.

The Spell of Beauty

After music, we are charmed by beauty. Nature is the primary arena for this type of magic. Flowers bloom and grow in a dazzling collection of colors. Mountains loom over the plains and we stand in awe of their majesty. Valleys and canyons cut a track through the earth and draw our gaze and wonder. The ocean stretches far beyond our gaze. The sun dances on the water and the waves crash in regular time. Snow glistens in the moonlight, illuminating the world. Forests loom large with each tree a tower of splendor, uniting to create a vast whole that stretches to the horizon. The world that God created is bursting with beauty and creation draws our eyes toward the Maker Himself.

Humans are made in the image of God which means

we have this creative spark within us as well. Artists capture beauty on canvas with paint. Sculptors unlock beauty from a block of stone. Writers create worlds of beauty in words which play on our mind's eyes. Poets speak truthfully about things that matter. All of this is beauty and all of it captures us in its spell. Beauty leads us on the paths of delight.

The Enchantment of Love

For many of us, beauty is a person. When that happens, we are in love. Love is the third thing that charms us. Lovers are often described as drunk or out of their minds. That is an enchantment if I ever heard of one.

Love is perhaps the deepest magic that God created in our world. Love is self-sacrificial. It is selfless. It would lead a parent to die for a child. It would lead God to die for humanity.

There is a sense of delight in love. Those who have fallen in love are delighted with one another. Furthermore, those in love find themselves more delighted in general, and not just with each other. Songs are more delightful. Food is more delightful. Nature is more delightful. Everything is more delightful when colored with love.

Find the Magic

Perhaps you do not feel very delighted right now. Perhaps the world is not a charming place to you. There is hope. This is where lament comes in. Lament is the first step back toward delight. Most people shy away from the sad songs, the cloudy days, and the lonely nights. But these things point to how things should be. When the music is sad, it points to the existence of joy. When the day is cloudy, the shadows point to the existence of the sun. Lonely nights show us that loneliness is not how we were created to live. We were made for community.

When we practice lament, we admit that we are not delighted. And God meets us in those valleys of shadows and death. Jesus spent Holy Saturday in the ground. He was and is delight, pure delight. And yet, for a time, that delight was cast out into the shadows.

But then delight reigned supreme. The grave was opened and death was undone. Delight won and sorrow lost. The first day of the new creation brought the delight of the risen Savior. Delight has the final say.

And in this in between time, between the Resurrection and the Second Coming, we find moments of delight in the normal magic of music, beauty, and love. These are the hints that true and ultimate delight is coming, and will come again.

ABOUT THE AUTHOR

N. K. Carlson is a writer living in Abilene, TX. He is originally from Libertyville, Illinois. He has degrees from the University of Illionois Urbana-Champaign and Logsdon Seminary. In addition to writing, he enjoys spending time with his wife Haley and his son, Andrew. You can find his work on Medium.

Made in the USA
Monee, IL
14 January 2020